an American ?

by Anne Miranda
illustrated by Sheffield Abella

Harcourt

Orlando   Boston   Dallas   Chicago   San Diego

Visit *The Learning Site!*

www.harcourtschool.com

Marta burst into her mother's office waving a piece of paper. "I have homework!" she shouted. She was more excited than usual.

Her mother looked away from her computer. "I've never seen you so interested in your homework before!" she laughed.

"This is really interesting homework," said Marta. "We are studying about citizenship in school. Did you know that my teacher, Mrs. Wong, didn't become a citizen until she was almost forty years old? She said she had to take a test. It must have been a hard test, if it took her forty years to study for it."

"Marta, you are so funny," her mother said. "Mrs. Wong didn't study for forty years. It takes a long time to become a citizen of the United States, but not that long. Mrs. Wong came from China. She had to live here for five years. Then she could petition, or ask, for citizenship. Everyone who comes here from another country has to wait that long. To become a citizen, the petitioners take a test. To pass the test, each petitioner has to speak English and know about our country. Then the petitioner promises to be loyal to the United States."

"That does sound difficult," said Marta. Then she asked, "Did I ever have to take the test?"

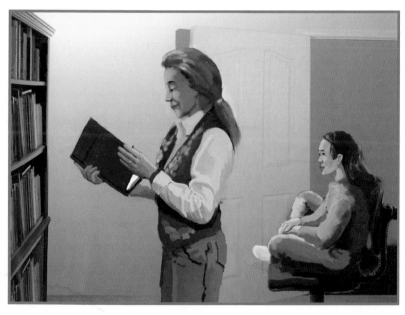

"No, you were born here. That means you are automatically a citizen of the United States," her mother answered.

"So, I'm an automatic American?" asked Marta. She wanted to be sure.

"Yes, you could say that," said her mother.

"What about Roberto? Did he have to take a test, or is he an automatic American, too?"

"He's automatic, just like you. You were born in Massachusetts. Roberto was born here in California," said Marta's mother. "I was born in Ohio. Your Grandma and Grandpa Jones were born in Kansas. Aunt Holly was born in Virginia. We are all automatic Americans."

"What about Daddy?" asked Marta.

"Well, your daddy is a naturalized citizen, like Mrs. Wong," said her mother.

"You mean Daddy came here from China?" asked Marta.

"No, that's not what I mean," her mother said. "I mean Daddy chose to be an American, like Mrs. Wong did.

"I'm sorry," her mother apologized. "I don't think anyone has told you about how Daddy came to America. It's an interesting story. I think it will help you understand how important citizenship is. Would you like to hear it?"

"Yes! I love stories," said Marta.

"Your daddy grew up in Cuba," her mother began. "Cuba is a warm country that is about 100 miles away from Florida. The people there speak Spanish. They have a government that is different from ours. Life in Cuba was very difficult for your grandfather and grandmother. They wanted to leave Cuba. They wanted to start a new life somewhere else. They asked their government for permission to leave Cuba. The government said they could not leave. They were obliged to stay."

"You mean a government can make you stay even if you want to leave?" asked Marta.

"In some countries, that's the way it is," said her mother. "In the United States, people are free to come and go as they like. They can stay or they can leave. That's one of the good things about being an American citizen."

"So, how did Daddy get out of Cuba?" asked Marta. She was very interested now.

"The government sent your grandparents a telegram. It said they had to stay in Cuba. However, your father could leave. So your grandparents had a difficult choice to make. Would they all stay in Cuba, or would they send their son—your father— to live in freedom?" said her mother.

7

"How could the government do that?" asked
Marta. "It's not fair to split up a family."

"It isn't fair," said her mother. "No one should
be faced with such a choice. I am glad I'll never
have that problem," she added. Then she gave
Marta a hug. "Your grandparents decided to send
your father to Spain. It was the best way to get him
out of the country. He was only fourteen, just a boy.
He was only a few years older than you are now.
Your grandparents put Daddy on the plane. They
weren't sure they would ever see him again."

"That is so sad," said Marta. "Was Daddy scared
to leave all by himself?"

"He was very scared!" said her mother. "Your grandparents made sure that someone met your daddy in Madrid. The man took your daddy to a camp. In the camp were many other Cuban boys. They had been sent to Spain by their parents. Every week, new boys came to stay at the camp. They waited until a family could take them in. Your daddy stayed there for about a year."

"He must have been very lonely there without his family," said Marta.

"It was a hard time for him. Daddy doesn't like to talk about it very much," Marta's mother told her.

"How did Daddy get here?" asked Marta.

"Your daddy's cousin found out that he was alone in Spain. She brought him to Florida to live with her."

"That was lucky for Daddy," said Marta.

Her mother smiled and nodded. "Your grandparents were allowed to leave Cuba about two years later. Your daddy and his cousin met your grandmother and grandfather at the airport in Miami. They couldn't believe how much your daddy had grown. What a happy day that was! Many families got together again that day. They were all happy. The sounds of joy resounded through the airport."

"I'm glad Daddy's family got together again!" said Marta.

"Everyone was glad," said her mother. "Soon after they arrived, your grandparents moved to Boston, Massachusetts. Your grandfather was able to find a job there. I met and married your daddy in Boston. You were born there."

"I still remember how cold the winter was in Boston. How did they stand it after living in Cuba where it is so hot?" asked Marta.

"They were happy to be together and living in freedom," her mother said. "They didn't mind the cold very much."

"Is freedom that important?" asked Marta.

"Yes, freedom is that important. Most people who have come to the United States have come to live in freedom. Here we have freedom of religion and freedom of speech. We have other freedoms, too. People in some parts of the world don't have these freedoms," said Marta's mother. "Our American citizenship guarantees them. People like Mrs. Wong and Daddy are grateful to be citizens of the United States. They know what it's like to live without the rights you and I were born with."

"I guess people who live in other places in the world think I'm pretty lucky," said Marta.

"Yes, you are very fortunate to be a citizen of the United States," said her mother.

"Mrs. Wong said that America is enriched by the different people who have come here," said Marta. "Did they all bring lots of money here?"

Marta's mother laughed. "Well, I guess a few lucky people came with money. Most people came to America with only the clothes they were wearing and a dream in their hearts. People who come to the United States do enrich our country. They bring their languages, their religions, and their foods. They also bring their art, their music, and their ideas."

"Does Daddy enrich America?" asked Marta.

"I think he does. He's an engineer. He helps to make roads and bridges. He gives his ideas and his hard work to our country," replied her mother.

"Hello," Daddy said, as he walked into the office.

"Oh, Daddy, you're home!" shouted Marta. She ran to give her father a big, tearful hug.

"What's this all about?" asked her father.

"Homework," said her mother, giving her husband a wink. "Marta is learning about citizenship."

"Oh, I see. Well, I became a citizen about a year after I married your mother. It was one of the most important, happiest days in my life," said Marta's father, smiling down at her.

"Did you take a test?" asked Marta.

"Of course. I had to prove I could speak English. I had to prove I knew about the government of the United States. I was a little nervous. However, the examiner was very kind. I did pass the test," said her father. "Would you like to see the certificate the examiner gave me?"

"Yes!" squealed Marta.

Marta's father took the certificate from a desk drawer. He showed it to Marta.

"Oh, Daddy. I am so glad you are free. I am so proud that you are an American," said Marta. She gave her father another big hug.

"What have you been telling this child?" Marta's father asked her mother.

"I told her how important freedom is. I told her why and how you came to the United States," said Marta's mother.

"I see," he said, looking into his daughter's teary eyes. "Marta, do you know another reason I came here?"

"No," said Marta.

"To be your father," he said. "I think that's the most important reason of all."

"Oh, Daddy," said Marta.